My Spectacular Self

Mimi Can't Camouflage

A Story About Avoiding Bias

by Jessica
Montalvo Jackson

illustrated by
Gal Weizman

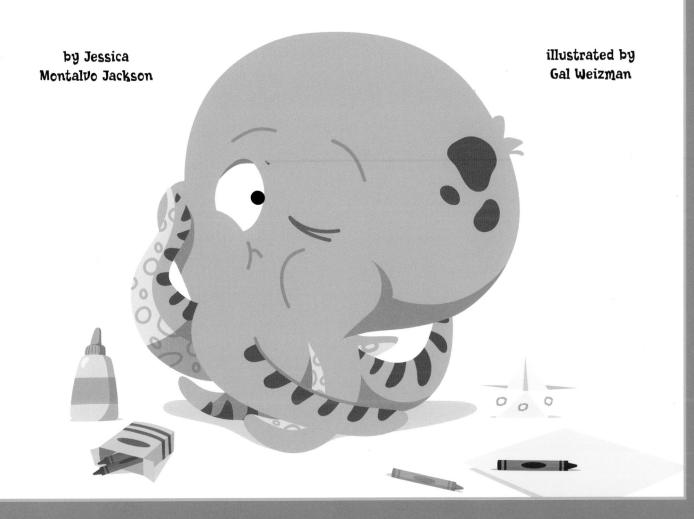

PICTURE WINDOW BOOKS
a capstone imprint

To my parents: One miracle led to another one,
and I'm forever thankful for your encouragement
you have given me from the day I was born.
Love you always. —JMJ

Published by Picture Window Books, an imprint of Capstone
1710 Roe Crest Drive, North Mankato, Minnesota 56003
capstonepub.com

Library of Congress Cataloging-in-Publication Data
Names: Jackson, Jessica Montalvo, author. | Weizman, Gal, illustrator.
Title: Mimi can't camouflage: a story about avoiding bias / by Jessica Montalvo Jackson;
illustrated by Gal Weizman. Other titles: Mimi can not camouflage
Description: North Mankato, Minnesota: Picture Window Books, [2023] | Series: My spectacular
self | Audience: Ages 5–7. | Audience: Grades K–1. | Summary: In her octopus kindergarten
class, little Mimi is the only one who can not change her color to camouflage, but when she gets
lost, she discovers that being small is sometimes an advantage.
Identifiers: LCCN 2021056914 (print) | LCCN 2021056915 (ebook) | ISBN 9781666340150
(hardcover) | ISBN 9781666340204 (paperback) | ISBN 9781666340273 (pdf) | ISBN
9781666340297 (kindle edition)
Subjects: LCSH: Octopuses—Juvenile fiction. | Camouflage(Biology)—Juvenile fiction. | Self-
confidence—Juvenile fiction. | CYAC: Octopuses—Fiction. | Camouflage (Biology)—Fiction. |
Self-confidence—Fiction. | Schools—Fiction. | LCGFT: Picture books.
Classification: LCC PZ7.1.J2745 Mi 2022 (print) | LCC PZ7.1.J2745 (ebook) | DDC [E]—dc23
LC record available at https://lccn.loc.gov/2021056914
LC ebook record available at https://lccn.loc.gov/2021056915

Special thanks to Amber Chandler for her consulting work.

Designed by Hilary Wacholz

Printed and bound in the USA. PO4882

Meet Mimi

HOBBIES: dancing, monkey bars at the playground, hanging out with friends

FAVORITE BOOKS: *Giraffes Can't Dance*

FAVORITE FOOD: oysters and shrimp

FUTURE GOALS: to become a teacher

GOALS FOR THIS YEAR
- PERFECT CAMOUFLAGE
- SPEAK UP MORE
- BECOME BRAVE

"Ready or not, here I come!" Mimi yelled. In the flick of a tentacle, Barbara disappeared.

Mimi searched around the schoolyard. She checked behind the swings and under the seesaw, but no luck.

I give up!

WOOSH! Barbara appeared! She was hiding on the slide the whole time.

"Barbara! You are the best at hide-and-seek," said Mimi.

"Thanks," said Barbara. "Your turn to hide, Mimi."

"Ready or not, here I come!" yelled Barbara.

"That was a world record, two seconds!" Barbara shouted.

Mimi always tried her best to hide, but her friends always found her right away.

In Mimi's kindergarten class, all the other octopi could change themselves to look like things you might find on the ocean floor.

Mimi tried so hard to camouflage . . .

. . . but nothing changed.

Mimi was the smallest octopus in her class. She wondered if that was why she couldn't camouflage.

"Ms. Peters, I hate being so small," Mimi told her teacher.

"You may be small, but you are mighty." Ms. Peters smiled as she hugged Mimi.

"I'm not!" Mimi cried. "I'm too little to be mighty. I'm too little to do anything. Especially camouflage!"

Before Ms. Peters could answer Mimi, the little octopus swam away.

Mimi's eyes filled with tears.

"Where are you going, Mimi?" her friends shouted. But Mimi just kept swimming.

Mimi couldn't see where she was going. She swam in circles and loops. When she finally stopped to take a break, Mimi didn't recognize where she was.

"Something doesn't feel right," Mimi said. Her tummy grumbled, and her tentacles were all wacky.

Then she saw it! A scary sea snake was swimming nearby.

Mimi hid behind some shells to stay safe. She was in serious danger.

Maybe if I'm quiet, the sea snake won't notice me.

Mimi closed her eyes, held her breath, and counted to five,
the way Barbara did before she changed during hide-and-seek.
Mimi squeezed her body tight, but still nothing changed.

When the sea snake wasn't looking, Mimi swam over to some brown and white coral. She lifted each tentacle and spread them in different directions to look like the coral around her. She closed her eyes and didn't move.

The sea snake tried searching for Mimi but couldn't see where she went.

The sea snake searched and searched, but it couldn't find Mimi. Finally, the sea snake gave up and swam away.

Mimi couldn't believe it. The snake never found her! She didn't change her skin color the way her friends did, but she could still hide. Her special skill was being super sneaky.

The next day, Mimi told her friends about her adventure. "I can't change my color to match a shell, like Barbara can. But I can make my body look like coral and stay still and quiet," Mimi explained.

"Yay, Mimi!" her friends cheered.

Mimi was smaller than her friends. And she couldn't change color the way they could. But now she knew that didn't mean she couldn't camouflage. She just needed to do it her own Mimi way.

Avoiding Bias

Bias is when we form an opinion about someone or something without a good reason. Bias can be positive or negative. For example, believing all tall people are good at basketball is a positive bias. Mimi formed a negative bias about herself. She believed she was too small to hide. Neither negative or positive biases are fair to others. To avoid bias, try to:

Remember that a person's size, age. skin color, or gender does not make them better or worse at ANYTHING!

Ask yourself WHY you like what you like.

Become aware of your biases.

Avoiding Bias Matters

1. In the story, Mimi formed a bias against her small size. Can you think of examples of other biases people might have?

2. Bias can be either positive or negative. What are some positive biases? Why should we avoid positive biases too?

3. How do you think Mimi felt when her friends laughed at her because she couldn't change her color?

4. Why is it important to not make fun of children who look or act differently than you?

5. Mimi overcame her challenge and found a way to hide. How do you think that made her feel? Do you think this will change how she thinks about herself and her abilities?

About the Author

Jessica Montalvo Jackson is an early childhood educator who has spent time in the classroom and as an administrator. In both her professional and personal life, she finds herself surrounded by and working with children. She followed in the footsteps of both of her parents, who also dedicated their lives to working with children and adults with special needs. Jessica believes that the foundation of any child's development has to stem from encompassing the qualities of being a good person: empathy and compassion, patience and love. Lots of her writing focuses on managing emotions and guiding her readers either through her own personal triumphs or relatable experiences.

About the Illustrator

Gal Weizman was born in Jerusalem, dreaming of flying above the white stone houses of her neighborhood like Peter Pan. As she grew older and became more acquainted with the laws of gravity, she had to abandon that plan. Instead, she devised a different way to never grow up: She attended Bezalel Academy of Arts and learned to draw. Gal loves to illustrate animals and creatures and to see her creations come to life. Her illustrations are bouncing through games and TV shows, sitting on packaging, and living in various children's books around the globe.